Bedtime Meditations for Children

The Magic of Trees

Ann Margaret Walsh

Bedtime Meditations for Children: The Magic of Trees
Copyright © 2025 Ann Margaret Walsh

Alderdawn Press

All rights reserved.

First Edition

ISBN: 978-1-7391826-2-5

Front Cover: 123rf.com/maryia777

Kara Wilson, Editor
www.emergingink.com

Without limiting the rights under copyright reserved above, no part of this publication may be reproduced, stored in or introduced into a retrieval system, or transmitted in any form or by any means (electronic, mechanical, photocopying, recording, or otherwise), without the prior written permission of the copyright owner.

OTHER BOOKS BY ANN MARGARET WALSH

Bedtime Meditations for Children

To my three wee saplings:
Willow, Hazel, & Rowan
For our love of trees.

Table of Contents

INTRODUCTION 1

MEDITATIONS FOR RELAXATION 9
MEDITATION 1: FALLING LEAF 11
MEDITATION 2: MOVEMENTS TO SLEEP 14
MEDITATION 3: TEDDY BEAR'S PICNIC 16
MEDITATION 4: MAGIC FOSSILS 20
MEDITATION 5: PAWPRINTS IN THE SNOW 24
MEDITATION 6: MEETING OF THE WATERS 28
MEDITATION 7: BE A TREE 32
MEDITATION 8: MURMURATION OF STARLINGS 35
MEDITATION 9: AUTUMN LEAVES 39
MEDITATION 10: FOREST DRAGONS 42
MEDITATION 11: THE FAIRY TREE 46

MEDITATIONS FOR UNLOCKING CREATIVITY 53
MEDITATION 12: BIRCH MOON 55
MEDITATION 13: FLOWER FRIENDS 58
MEDITATION 14: FAIRY DOORS 61
MEDITATION 15: WOODLAND ADVENTURE 65
MEDITATION 16: WAND WOOD 67
MEDITATION 17: SNAIL TRAIL 71
MEDITATION 18: A WALK THROUGH AN ENCHANTED FOREST .. 75
MEDITATION 19: MONKEY PUZZLE 78
MEDITATION 20: ALPINE FOREST 81
MEDITATION 21: YOUR VERY OWN TREE ADVENTURE 84

Introduction

I first created meditational stories for my children to help lower their anxiety levels, promote relaxation, and tap into positive thinking and creativity just before bedtime. I aimed to open a unique space for them within which we could bond and explore the depths of their imaginations. *Bedtime Meditations for Children: The Magic of Trees* is the second book in the Bedtime Meditations for Children series.

The Magic of Trees

Trees have been on our planet for millions of years. They are the dominant life force within forests, upon which many ecosystems depend. Trees not only provide oxygen, but they also improve air quality, making them one of the most precious resources on Earth.

The Celts believed specific species of trees carried certain powers and meanings. Some of the meditations in this book draw on Celtic tree mythology to introduce messages of self-worth and to add a little magic.

Walks with your children through local woodlands during the day can increase physical and mental health, activate the five senses, enable them to practice mindfulness, and expose them to colour therapy. Many studies show that children are happier, healthier, less stressed, and more creative when they're connected to the natural world. So, why not step into the enchanting forest of your child's imagination to experience the amazing benefits such stimulation can bring?

What Is Guided Meditation?

Guided meditation helps someone create a mental image that focuses the mind in a particular direction. The goals of the meditations are to improve sleep, reduce stress and anxiety, build strong mental wellness, and unlock creativity.

How Does It Work?

Through guided meditation and the soothing sound of a trusted voice, children can slowly be introduced to mindfulness and taught how to harness the power of their imagination. Meditation cultivates a healthy lifestyle by promoting relaxation, improving sleep, reducing stress, building resilience, and unlocking creativity. Let's more closely examine each of those.

Promotes relaxation

Through gentle adventure, little ones are brought on a unique journey to a special space filled with tranquillity.

Improves sleep

It can sometimes be difficult to settle children in bed at night. Perhaps they are restless, anxious, or just uneasy about falling asleep on their own. Creating a happy and peaceful space at bedtime can make all the difference.

Guided meditation can reduce the likelihood of sleep disturbances experienced during rapid cognitive development by helping your child drift into a peaceful slumber. Sleep disruption may present itself in the form of nightmares, which can create an uneasy environment and make it difficult for children to settle. Take the focus away from the cycle of frightening and disruptive scenes and shine light upon calming, positive thoughts by engaging your child in guided meditation.

Reduces stress and anxiety

Stress and anxiety are real problems in today's world and are affecting children more and more from a young age. Any number of triggers can set off a child's inner restlessness, but giving them the tools to deal with worrying or frightening thoughts can make all the difference.

Through practice, it is possible to learn how to stop the constant flow of thoughts and to work through issues that cause stress. Wouldn't it be wonderful to fall asleep without anxiety and wake up the next day well-rested, refreshed, and full of energy?

Builds resilience

Building a strong sense of self-worth and confidence during childhood is paramount. A child believing in their abilities, acknowledging how special they are, and having resounding faith in the love of their friends and family is more likely to have unwavering mental fortitude that sees them through the hardships of life. It is one of the best gifts a parent can give a child.

Unlocks creativity

Fast-paced living can make it difficult to find time for nurturing the creative process. Dedicating just ten or fifteen minutes a night to creative thinking will result in a noticeable difference.

By accessing the creative part of their minds, children can learn to problem solve, an excellent life skill to possess. Children can mould and create a whole new world by utilising their imagination. Once they enter "the flow," they can unlock a myriad of desirable life skills.

How Do I Introduce Meditation to My Child?

The meditations in this book work best for children ages three to ten, but it depends on the child. I have provided a recommended age for each meditation; you can alter the language to suit your child.

When introducing a new meditation, take the time to answer questions and explain the meanings of unfamiliar words so the child is comfortable with the language being used. It is best to stick with one meditation for a couple of weeks before proceeding to a new one. This allows the child to relax into it and to be able to fully enjoy it through familiarity.

At the end of your usual bedtime routine, switch off the main light and leave the door ajar to allow soft light to filter in from another room. A night light, salt lamp, or a dimmed desk lamp would also work well in the bedroom.

Before starting the meditation, ask the child to close their eyes. When speaking, use a low, soothing voice and allow long pauses to give the child time to imagine different elements and to build the scene in their mind.

The Inclusion of Siblings

Both the meditations for relaxation and the meditations for unlocking creativity can be shared by siblings in the same room. For the latter, each sibling can simply take a turn to answer the same question. Sometimes this can result in bigger, better ideas being gently bounced between the children. It can be a wonderful experience for siblings to share. "Meditation 6: Meeting of the Waters" is written specifically for siblings and explores sibling love and friendship.

There are huge benefits to be gained and there is no time like the present to embark on these adventures through, around, and with trees—so let's get started!

Meditations for Relaxation

Meditations for Relaxation

The Benefits of Relaxation Meditations

These meditations not only help your child relax, but they introduce different adventures that can build a strong sense of self-worth and confidence. This sets the foundation for a deeper inner calm and an innate ability to better manage emotions. Through gentle adventure, wrap your little one in a blanket of tranquillity to aid in a peaceful night's slumber.

Additional Relaxation Techniques

Additional techniques can be used to help your child relax.

A breathing exercise can be carried out at the beginning of each meditation. Focus on breathing slowly in through the nose and out through the mouth to calm the nervous system and help the body let go of stress.

A gentle head, foot, or hand massage can improve relaxation and help settle the child for a peaceful night's sleep.

If your child is experiencing difficulty drifting off to sleep post-meditation, you can introduce ten minutes of their favourite calming music afterwards or play a track of nature sounds relevant to the meditation such as birds' songs, river sounds, or rainfall.

Positive Reinforcements

Children need to hear how treasured, important, and unique they are. Encouraging them to tap into their strengths boosts their self-esteem. Within these relaxation meditations, a nurturing and supportive environment is created that fosters growth and confidence. Common themes found in positive reinforcement include but are not limited to self-empowerment, the embracing of sibling love, strong familial bonds, friendship, blossoming talents, the acceptance of differences, the acknowledgement of change, and the release of worries or fears.

Meditation 1
Falling Leaf

Guide Age: 3+
Themes: Forests, mindfulness, being part of nature, love
Concepts: Leaves, nature, wind, autumn

This short meditation is set in a serene woodland and promotes relaxation by exploring what it might be like to be a leaf drifting gently on an autumn breeze. Mindfulness is explored by focusing on the colours, shapes, and sizes of the leaves. The element of family is introduced to promote warmth, safety, and security, enabling a seamless shift into a serene slumber where vividly colourful dreams are sure to follow.

Close your eyes.
Feel your head sink into the softness of your pillow.
Take a deep breath…
In through your nose…
And out through your mouth.
In through your nose…
And out through your mouth.

Feel your body become more and more relaxed.
It is autumn and the leaves on the trees are changing colours.
You see rusty reds, burnt oranges, golden browns, and sunshine yellows.
Imagine you are a leaf on one of those trees.
Now think about what colour you are…
What shape you are…
What size you are…

A gust of wind blows through the branches of the trees making them sway,
and the leaves jiggle.
Feel yourself move with this breeze,
swaying this way and that until…
You finally break free from the branch
and are carried on the light wind.
Up and up into the air you go,
swirling,
gliding,
floating.

Feel your body relax
as you drift through the air.

Down below you,
as the sun sets,
you see different woodland animals
on their way to their nests.
A red squirrel scurries up an oak tree into its drey,
a red fox leaps through the fallen leaves on the way to its den,
a hedgehog disappears into its house of wood and leaves,
a badger enters its sett in the hedgerows.
Take a moment to think of any other animals you might see making their way to their homes for the night.

You are floating down to the forest floor now…
Feel yourself land gently among the other leaves.

Now, imagine those leaves to be family and friends.
You are surrounded by their love.
Know how much you are cherished and loved
as you drift off to sleep tonight.
One… two… three…
It is now time for sleep.
Goodnight and sleep tight!

Meditation 2

Movements to Sleep

Guide Age: 3+
Themes: Relaxation, sleepiness, beginner meditation
Concepts: Bedtime rest, body awareness

This meditation introduces children to mindfulness and promotes deep relaxation. It can be used as a standalone piece or be introduced at the end of any of the other relaxation meditations.

Close your eyes…
And take a deep breath…
In through your nose…
And out through your mouth.
In through your nose…
And out through your mouth.

Take a moment to feel your belly slowly rise and fall with each breath that you take…

Sleepiness is now beginning to travel up through your body…
Moving from your toes to the soles of your feet and onto the heels…
Moving up through your ankles to your calves,
up to your knees, then your thighs.
Your legs feel very sleepy now, very light and relaxed…
The sleepiness continues to travel up to your hips,

reaching your back and your shoulders,
flowing down into your arms…
Reaching your elbows, your wrists, and the palms of your hands…
Flowing down into your fingers and then to your thumbs.
Your arms are feeling very sleepy now… very light and relaxed…

The sleepiness continues to travel up to your neck…
Reaching your head,
then flowing to your cheeks, to your ears, and onto your temples…

Moving on to your forehead, to your nose, and your eyes…
Your eyelids feel very sleepy now…
The sleepiness travels down your eyelashes, finally pulling your eyelids shut tight.
One… two… three…
It is now time for sleep…
Goodnight and sleep tight!

Meditation 3
Teddy Bear's Picnic

Guide Age: 3+
Themes: Making new friends, having fun outdoors
Concepts: Flowers, woodland, nature, picnic, meadow, bears

This meditation is set in a serene meadow and woodland. The summer flowers play music, celebrating the vibrancy of the season and creating a joyful yet calming atmosphere.

This meditation reminds children that new friendships can be found when they least expect them. This is the perfect meditation to do after a wildflower-identifying woodland walk in summer. You can substitute the flowers in this meditation with native flowers familiar to the child.

Close your eyes…
And take a deep breath…
In through your nose…
And out through your mouth.
In through your nose…
And out through your mouth.

Imagine you are walking through a beautiful meadow...
The buttercups, daisies, and grasses are beautifully overgrown

and reach up to your waist.
You can feel the feathery seeded grass tips
tickle your hands as you make your way across the meadow.

The buttercups shine golden yellow in the sunlight
and reflect their light upon you,
bringing you feelings of happiness and warmth.
Let this happiness wash over you for a moment…

Up ahead, you see a gate.
This gate is the entrance to a woodland.
The wood is dusted with the colour of beautiful blooms.
Small pink Herb Robert wildflowers peep out from the hedgerows
while cow parsley and yarrow add speckles of white.
It is summer, and the trees have bountiful leaves
that canopy the woodland floor.
Foxgloves stretch up, seeking the dappled light.
The sweet scent of honeysuckle fills the air.

Take a moment to breathe in the scent of the nature that is around you…

You see a path that leads you through a carpet of bluebells.
A tiny stream flows past, its current gurgling against rocks;
leaves and petals bob along at a quickening pace.
You step over the water to continue your journey.

The undergrowth ahead of ferns, brambles, and nettles is
so dense that you cannot continue.
You are about to turn back when
suddenly you see a pawprint on a tree.
You press your hand against it,
and when you look up, the undergrowth parts!

You step through into a circled clearing…
Only to find several groups of brown bears
sitting on blankets wearing colourful shirts and funny hats!

Take a moment to imagine what they look like...
Some might have stars or spots on their shirts and hats,
some shirts might be frilly,
some hats might be pointy or round

One of the smaller bears beckons for you to join them
on their blanket.
You sit beside them.
They open a basket to take out their food.
"Can you guess what's inside?" the bear asks.
Take a moment now to think what might be in the basket...

Bear takes out white iced cupcakes with sprinkles
and fruits the colour of a rainbow... strawberries, oranges, pineapple slices, apples, blueberries, and blackberries...
"My favourite is honey cake!" the bear chuckles. "And lemonade, of course!"
"Don't forget the sandwiches," says a bigger bear in a deep voice.
Sandwiches, ones with your favourite fillings, are then laid out in front of you.

After the picnic, the bears arrange themselves in a circle
and, holding hands, begin to move clockwise.
A melodic tune gently plays.
You look around to discover that the flowers are playing the music!
The honeysuckles are trumpeting.
The foxgloves are piping.
The bluebells are ringing.
The daisies are jingling.
The violets and Herb Roberts are humming.
Imagine what other flowers might join in...
(*Orchid, gorse, nightshade, campion, dog rose?*)

The bears move in rhythm to the tune.
Each time the music stops, the bears try to pause their dancing too.
When a bear fails to stop, they skip out of the ring of undergrowth until finally just you and your bear friend are left.

You give each other a hug
and you promise to visit again soon.

You leave the ring and make your way back through the woodland
to the meadow of daisies and buttercups.

As you walk through the meadow,
the sweet scent from the daisies
fills you with comfort, joy, and peace.
You begin to feel your eyes grow heavy,
and your body becomes very relaxed.

Drift off to sleep now thinking of the happy time
you had with your new friend bear…

One… two… three…
It is now time for sleep…
Goodnight and sleep tight!

Meditation 4
Magic Fossils

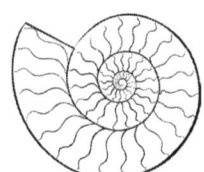

Guide Age: 4+
Themes: Magic, forest, fossils, exploration, scientific research
Concepts: Earth, nature, animals, dinosaurs, the past, extinction, palaeontology

This meditation is for tiny explorers as they are presented with the opportunity to travel back to the exciting time of the dinosaur. Children are introduced to animals that existed in the past and its ecosystems. An appreciation for our planet is fostered and a deep-rooted respect for animals is nurtured.

Children are fascinated by poo and even more so by dinosaur poo! In this meditation, they become a scientist and are tasked with solving the mystery of the producer of the poo.

There is an opportunity for the child to return to the adventure another night to select one of the other fossils for a completely new adventure. They could travel back in time to see ammonites or a megalodon or they could uncover a fossilised bone of a dodo, transporting them to the island of Mauritius hundreds of years ago. This adventure can be inspired by their own interests in prehistoric animals.

Close your eyes…
And take a deep breath…
In through your nose…
And out through your mouth.
In through your nose…
And out through your mouth.

A white box appears in your mind.
Carefully focus on this box for a moment.
Notice the tall four sides,
the tight lid.
Watch now as it slowly begins to change colour.
Then change to another colour…
And another…
Could this be a magic box?
You must open it to find out!
Take your time to slowly lift the lid…
Inside you find lots of objects
in many different shapes and sizes.
There are ammonites, which are tiny shell creatures (cephalopods)
That lived in the ocean millions of years ago;
there is also a large tooth—could it be from a megalodon (an extinct shark-like creature)?
Or a *Tyrannosaurus rex*?
There are also rocks in the box...
You study these for a moment and then pick up the largest one.
It is heavy.
Suddenly there is a flash of bright light.

You have been transported to a forest!
The rock in your hands feels different now…
Warmer.
Softer.
A pungent smell wafts up your nose.
Is it poo?
You drop it once you realise what it is.
It *is* poo!

Your mission now is to find the producer of this poo.
You have become a scientist!

Thump! Thump!

The ground shakes.
The vibrations move up through the soles of your feet.
You peek through the giant ferns to see what it could be…
A *Triceratops* has stopped to munch on some plants.
Could this be the producer of the poo?
Take a moment to watch this magnificent creature with its head frill and three horns.
It releases a large poo but it looks different from the one you once held.
You follow the *Triceratops* farther into the forest to continue exploring, keeping close to the dense foliage as you move so as not to be seen.

There is a roar.
Up ahead you see an *Ankylosaurus*,
Another plant-eating dinosaur.
Take a moment to observe this unusual creature
with its wide head and large, club-like tail.
It releases a poo!
Perhaps this is the poo producer you are looking for?
But it also looks different…
The *Ankylosaurus* slowly moves away,
carrying the weight of its mighty armour of bony plates and spikes.

As you approach a clearing, you see a great moving shadow,
and then the owner of the shadow…
It is a *Tyrannosaurus rex*!
Could this giant carnivorous dinosaur be the producer of the poo?
Suddenly, it releases an enormous poo. It looks a lot like the one you held earlier!
By studying poo, you can learn what a dinosaur ate,
what illness it may have had,

and where it lived.
But there's no time for analysis now!
Raptors suddenly run through bushes, and the T-rex gives chase.

It is time to find the poo you dropped earlier
so you can return home.
You walk back to find the spot where you first entered the forest.
There it is! Glistening in the sunlight.
The poo you dropped is beginning to turn back into rock.
You pick up the fossilised poo—called coprolite—
and are transported back to the magic box in the present time.
You place the coprolite back into the box with the other fossils.

Perhaps you might return to the magic box some other night
and choose one of the other fossils.
But for tonight, your adventure is over.

All this time travelling has made you feel very sleepy.
Your body is becoming lighter.
Feel your head sinking into the soft pillow.
Magnificent dreams of exploration and time travel await you now in dreamland…

One… two… three…
It is now time for sleep…
Goodnight and sleep tight!

Meditation 5

Pawprints in the Snow

Guide Age: 3+
Themes: Family, interconnectedness, adventure, winter
Concepts: Snow, snowprints, nature, trees, birds, badgers

    This meditation is set in the snowy countryside. The white backdrop of snow creates a peaceful and calming atmosphere, providing a chance to connect with the beauty of nature in winter. The woodland animals bring life; the alder symbolises strength and balance; animal tracks encourage an adventure into the unknown.

    The falling snowflake exercise within the meditation leads the child into a restful state and calms their body and mind. This exercise can also be used as a standalone piece.

Close your eyes…
And take a deep breath…
In through your nose…
And out through your mouth.
In through your nose…
And out through your mouth.

You find yourself walking in the countryside on a blanket of freshly fallen snow…

Your feet sink softly into the snow
with each step that you take,
leaving only your footsteps behind you…

You notice pawprints ahead.
You decide to follow them!
They lead you to a cottage,
where you see a puppy
prancing playfully around the garden with a child.

Then you spot another set of pawprints.
As you follow them along a path
you spy a flash of red up ahead—a fox!
It scampers away.

On the roadside, you notice an alder tree dusted in white,
as if covered with icing.
Its tiny cones, dark brown, peering out from the snow…

You can hear birds singing high up from a hollow…
Whistling,
and warbling,
and chattering aloud.
A bird flies down to a nearby branch,
its dark feathers are speckled white…
It is a starling!
As the starling sings,
snowflakes begin to fall.

Imagine you are one of those falling snowflakes.
Feel your body become lighter and lighter as
you drift down from the sky,
Weightless and free.
And as you fall,
allow your arms and legs to become relaxed.
Let this calm feeling spread through your body now
and take a deep breath in through your nose,

and out through your mouth.
You gently land on the carpet of snow in the woodland.
Take a moment to rest
before you reform into yourself again.

It is time to continue your journey through the snow…

There are more animal tracks up ahead…
What animal could it be?
Could it be a squirrel? No, the tracks are too big.
Could it be a bear? No, the tracks are too small.
Five toes, broad paws and claws…
Can you guess what animal left these tracks?

Follow the tracks through the snow to find out…

They lead you into a woodland,
then wind around a horse chestnut tree,
weaving past a group of hazel saplings,
and continuing beyond the shiny spiky holly tree
that sprawls and spills onto the pathway.

The tracks disappear by a hedgerow and lead
to an underground burrow.
A badger has gone back to their sett.
It is here where they sleep during the day.

These burrows are passed down from generation to generation.
The badger's parents, grandparents, and great-grandparents
dug out the tunnels and added to the sett over many years.
And they all raised their young in this very burrow!
Just like the badgers' ancestors, our ancestors have contributed greatly to the way we live today.

Take a moment to think of the little cubs,
all curled up in their nest underground
with their mum and dad,

feeling safe and happy with their family,
kept warm by dried leaves and grass.

Imagine you are one of those cubs now
curled up with your family,
cosy and warm,
away from the snow.
Drifting off into a dreamy night's sleep…

Sweet dreams, little cub.

One… two… three…
It is now time for sleep…
Goodnight and sleep tight!

Meditation 6
Meeting of the Waters

Guide Age: 5+
Themes: Rivers, sibling rivalry, colour symbolism
Concepts: Fish, nature, love, wish

This adventure begins at the banks of a river surrounded by the lush greenery of nature. This meditation will evoke feelings of calm, relaxation, and revitalisation and foster a positive mindset.

The two rivers in this meditation symbolise the different paths in life that siblings are on. While travelling these paths, they will each undergo unique experiences. The merging of the rivers into one signifies how they can come together to support each other in their different experiences and be happy for each other's accomplishments.

In this guided meditation, relationships between siblings (insert brothers and/or sisters as appropriate to match the child's family) are celebrated and the idea of sibling rivalry is explored. The positive messages of sibling love and friendship reinforce strong relationships during the day and introduce the idea that memories of the past are shared, future memories are to be cherished, and the present moment is to be celebrated together.

Close your eyes…
And take a deep breath…
In through your nose…
And out through your mouth.
In through your nose…
And out through your mouth.

Imagine you are walking barefoot along the banks of a small river…

Feel the soft blades of grass
caress your feet with each step that you take.

Notice the colour green.

Green grass underfoot as soft as a pillow;
green leaves on the oak, the hazel, and the willow;
green moss on the rocks at the riverside;
green ferns and green plants growing freely alongside.

Take a moment to soak up the serene, green nature
that surrounds you.
Breath in calm…
Then, breathe out.
Feel your body begin to relax.
Let your mind quieten.

It's time to return to the river…

You are no longer alone on this walk.
You can feel your *sister's* hand in yours.
Her hand feels warm,
and you feel happy that you are together.

You love your *sister*
and *she* loves you.
Best friends who share a unique bond,
you are walking through this life together,

sharing your past, your present, and your future.
And sharing this adventure.

The hillside above is covered with tall trees
that stretch up to the sky.
They are watching over the valley
and water beneath.
Surprisingly, you notice that there is not one river,
but two!
You decide to follow the smaller river,
And your *sister* follows the larger one.
You lose sight of your *sister*
as your rivers meander in different directions.

Tune into the sounds of the river now.
You can hear it bubbling and gurgling
as it flows over the rocks.
Watch the water
as it gushes forward.
Notice the tiny golden fish jump up,
breaking the surface of the water
before diving back in again.
You have never seen a more beautiful fish.
Take a moment to make a wish!

Eventually, you reach a point where the two rivers meet.
Up ahead, you see your *sister* waiting to greet you
at the mouth of the new larger river.
You are filled with a mixture of emotions.
At first, you wish you arrived there before *her*,
but then you see how happy *she* is
and you feel yourself become happy for *her*.
She looks delighted to see you.
You realise that no one arrived first,
and no one arrived last.
You both just arrived when the time was right for each of you.

You both took a different path that led you to that location at different times.
Had you not stopped to see the golden fish,
Then you would have missed out
on that moment of marvel and your wish!
You step forward
and hug your *sister*.
Then, you both watch the two rivers
as they join to form the larger river.
Flowing forward, they came together
at the right moment.
And they are faster
and stronger together now as one.
Just like you and your *sister*.

Love each other…
Care for each other…
Be happy for each other in your accomplishments
and keep each other close…
And you will always have each other.
Sisters… best friends forever.

You can hear the river ripple
and gurgle as it flows forward…
It's making you feel sleepy.
Listen to the sounds of the river
As you drift off to sleep.

One… two… three…
It is now time for sleep…
Goodnight and sleep tight!

Meditation 7

Be a Tree

Guide Age: 4+
Themes: Forests, mindfulness, being part of nature, loved ones
Concepts: Tree, nature, weather, love

This meditation allows the child to tap into their imagination and visualise themselves as a tree. By becoming a tree, the child will experience nature-connectedness. When we perceive ourselves as a part of nature, we learn that we are fundamentally connected to everything and develop a deep-rooted love and respect for all life, choosing from that moment on to nurture and protect it.

Concepts such as standing tall with confidence and feeling grounded are introduced. Like the tree withstanding all weathers, children can look inside themselves for the strength they need when emotions are running strong. The tree does not stand alone; it is part of a forest family that supports it. This feeling of family support is carried with the child into their daily lives.

Close your eyes…
And take a deep breath…
In through your nose…
And out through your mouth.
In through your nose…
And out through your mouth.

Think of your favourite tree.
Imagine you *are* that tree…

Take a moment to visualise your trunk, your branches, and the shape of your leaves…

Imagine now that the sun is shining down upon you, warming your leaves, giving you light and strength to grow.
Feel positive energy flowing into your branches
and then into your trunk,
nourishing you with happiness and love,
making you feel a deep sense of contentment.

Now visualise your surroundings.
You are part of a wild and fantastic forest.
Your family and friends are all trees within this forest too.
Take a moment to think of them.
Perhaps they are an oak, an elm, or a sycamore…
You decide.
Feel their energies as you stand tall and strong together.
In this forest, just as in your real life,
you are surrounded by those who love you.

A gentle breeze passes through your leaves,
making them rustle.
As the breeze picks up into a light wind,
you feel your branches move.
Let your branches stretch to the sky toward the sun…

Branches are designed to bend and sway in the wind,
to withstand any gusts.
As the wind grows stronger,
feel your roots spread deeper into the earth,
stretching farther and farther under the soil,
running across the forest floor.
These roots anchor you,
keeping you grounded and safe.
No matter what weather is happening around you,
you will be okay.
You can stand strong.
You belong to this Earth and are part of its nature.

Be happy with who you are
because you are important.
This world needs you
because you are destined to do great things in the future
to make this world an even better place.

The wind slows and you begin to feel relaxed.
Feel calmness move throughout your body.

Take a moment to pay attention to your breath.
Breathing in and breathing out…
Notice how light and relaxed your body feels…
Invite sleep to come to you…

And as you drift off, imagine being with your tree family and friends, visualising what trees they might be…

One… two… three…
It is now time for sleep…
Goodnight and sleep tight!

Meditation 8
Murmuration of Starlings

Guide Age: 5+
Themes: Flying, birds, friendship
Concepts: starlings, nature, love, friends

Take to the skies in this meditation and experience what it might be like to fly as a starling in a murmuration—when thousands of starlings swoop and swirl in planes and waves in the sky. Murmuration mirrors the trust that is shared between friends.

Friendships can be challenging to navigate at times. Sometimes a friendship might last forever, sometimes it might end due to a particular reason: physical distance, growing apart, or even unexpectedly for an unknown reason. But it's important to know that no matter if a friend is physically with us or not, they will continue to be a part of our lives through the happy experiences we shared, living on as treasured memories within us. And there is always a chance that friends can reconnect again in the future.

The sensation of flying helps the child to relax and drift off into a peaceful night's sleep.

Close your eyes…
And take a deep breath…
In through your nose…
And out through your mouth.
In through your nose…
And out through your mouth.

Imagine a starling…
With its dark feathers and speckles of white…
Now, look more closely at the dark feathers and see the iridescence of colour…
Hues of purple, green, and even pink shine through…
The feathers are like a colourful galaxy of stars.

Imagine now that you are that starling.
Look down at your thin pink legs.
You can see your tiny feet gripping a tree branch.

Suddenly, you hear thousands of starlings calling out.
They want you to join them in the sky!
Open your wings and take flight.
Fly up to the sky to join them.

As you flap your wings, you feel happy and free.
When you reach a great height,
take a moment to really open your wings and glide through the air.
Feel the sense of calm this brings you
and let your body relax.

You have joined the flock of starlings now in the sky.
Imagine this flock is made up of all your friends!
All the friends you have met throughout your life…

Friends you might see every day,
Friends who might have gone away,
Friends you met on holidays,
Friends who may no longer play,

Friends who have fun things to say,
Friends you've yet to meet some day.

Know that just like this starling,
you will always be surrounded by your friends.
Some friends might fly away for a while,
then they might fly back.
Or they might never return.
And that's okay.
Friends will always keep a place in your heart.

Soar with your starling friends now
in a murmuration to decorate the skies.

Watch the six birds closest to you…
See how you can change direction quickly and easily
without bumping into them.
By working together with your friends,
you can move
to create beautiful shapes in the sky,
having fun and making beautiful memories
that will last forever in your heart.

It's time to make some shapes!
First make the shape of a leaf.
See how it looks as if it's tossing in the wind
as you all dart this way and that in the sky.

Think about what other shapes you might make…
Maybe a beating heart…
A rolling ball…
Or another pretty, moving pattern…

Take a moment now to imagine making some more of these shapes
in the sky.

Lastly, together, you create the shape of a huge flying bird.

Each of the starlings, one by one,
fly away to their roosts for the night.
As you return to your tree,
you feel your body become relaxed.
Take time to settle in your warm nest for the night.
You are tired and ready to rest.

Drift off to sleep now thinking of all those wondrous shapes in the sky.

One… two… three…
It is now time for sleep…
Goodnight and sleep tight!

Meditation 9
Autumn Leaves

Guide Age: 4+
Themes: Forests, mindfulness, autumn
Concepts: Tree, nature, rights of nature, forest bathing, leaves

Autumn brings change to the forest. Change can be challenging for a child to deal with. A positive message regarding change sets the foundation for a child's coping skills and helps them understand that change is not to be feared but to be seen as an opportunity for growth. The falling, swirling leaves will lull your child into a peaceful night's sleep. Vivid and beautiful autumn-coloured dreams are sure to follow.

Close your eyes…
And take a deep breath…
In through your nose…
And out through your mouth.
In through your nose…
And out through your mouth.

Rusty-red, burnt-orange, and golden-brown leaves
release from the canopy of trees high above you.
They cascade down in a hurrying flurry,
as if they are dancing to the tune of the autumn breeze
through the trees.
Leaves land playfully on your shoulders,
some adorn your hair, taking the shape of a crown.
This forest, wild, wonderful, and magical
is yours to appreciate and explore.

More leaves fall, landing softly on the ground to
create a warm quilt for the forest floor.
You can feel the soft leaves under your bare feet.
The warmth from the earth beneath them
travels up through the soles of your feet and into your body,
healing and recharging your energy.
Feel your body begin to relax as this healing warmth spreads
to your legs and to your tummy,
flowing then into your arms and your hands
until it reaches your neck and head.
Your entire body is completely relaxed now,
bathed in this healing warmth.

The leaves continue to fall all around you.
The forest is changing colour for a short time to crimson and gold.
All the green that will remain will be of the evergreen trees,
the ground plants, and the moss.

To your left is the fallen trunk of an oak tree
taken down by a storm. Patches of moss grow on it.
Reach out and touch the moss with your fingertips
and notice how soft and spongy it feels.

Mushroom caps have sprung up
to feast on the decomposing wood.
Things are changing in the forest.
Like the changes happening in the forest,

there might be some changes happening in your life.
Think of something that has changed for you…
(Perhaps it's gaining a new sibling, starting school or transferring to another one, making a new friend, starting a new activity, moving to a new home…)

Change may be welcomed,
or may seem scary.
Sometimes you want change to happen,
sometimes you don't.
But change will always bring good things with it,
even if you can't see what those good things might be at first.

Sometimes change can be beautiful like
the leaves changing colour in autumn.
Sometimes change can leave you feeling vulnerable
like the bare trees having lost their leaves by winter.

The leaves that have fallen on the forest floor
after being broken down
will eventually pass nutrients back to the roots of the trees,
giving them energy, and so, helping them grow.
They produce new leaves in spring.

Change will happen throughout your life.
Just remember that change enables you to experience new things
and to grow.

As you continue your walk through the forest,
look up and watch the leaves
float down from the sky.
See their different shapes and colours.
Watch them drift down
until you fall into a snug and serene sleep.

One… two… three…
It is now time for sleep…
Goodnight and sleep tight!

Meditation 10
Forest Dragons

Guide Age: 4+
Themes: Dragons, family, exploration, discovery
Concepts: Forest dragons, oak trees, nature, love

Discover the magical world of the forest dragons, who inhabit the ancient forests of Ireland. Meet the elusive, fierce, and yet gentle oak dragon and watch how it cares for its babies. See how the young dragons flourish under the wisdom and guidance of their mother while venturing out to explore the ancient forest where they live.

Why not visit the forest dragons another night to see a red copper beech tree dragon or a rare blackthorn dragon?

Close your eyes…
And take a deep breath…
In through your nose…
And out through your mouth.
In through your nose…
And out through your mouth.

Tonight, you will go in search of the forest dragons
who live deep in the ancient forests of Ireland.
They are friendly, as all Irish dragons are.

Now, imagine you are exploring in one of those ancient forests…

Leaves rustle and twigs snap under your feet as you walk.
Up ahead, you notice an oak tree
with golden-green leaves glinting in the sunlight.
The bark of the trunk is blanketed in a yellow-green moss
that stretches up as far as its lower branches.

You gently stroke the moss…
It feels soft,
and spongey,
and warm.
Suddenly, the tree begins to move and transform
before your very eyes!
You have discovered…
A forest dragon! An oak tree dragon!

Forest dragons are hard to find
and have only been seen by a few very lucky explorers.
That's because when these majestic creatures hear noises in the forest, they immediately hide
by taking the shape of trees, standing still,
only to sway in the wind if they need to blend in
with the moving forest.

Watch the oak dragon
as it uncurls its tail
and you will see what it is protecting.
There are three coloured eggs each with a golden shimmer.
You touch the eggs.
They are warm.
All tucked up and nestled in a pile of colourful leaves.

Crack, crack, crack…

The eggs begin to open.
Step back!

Pop, Pop, Pop…

Three little heads pop up,
Each with shimmering gold scales.

The baby dragons cautiously look around before
smashing out of their eggs with their feet.
Mother Dragon rushes to help them,
but they push her back.
They want to explore this new world on their own.
Mother Dragon must watch over them to keep them safe
but she must also allow them to explore
and uncover the curiosities of the forest for themselves.

Just like Mother Dragon,
I am here to help and guide you,
to teach you about dangers and how to stay safe.
I will teach you all that I know so
you can look after yourself when you are older.
All young creatures start out as explorers,
learning first about their surroundings
before gathering knowledge.

Elders, such as parents, aunts, uncles, and grandparents
have so much knowledge.
It's important to listen carefully
when they share their own stories.

The baby oak dragons chase after their mother,
tumbling on the forest floor,
jumping over tree stumps,
and sniffing the woody-scented air.

Could they be picking up your scent?

A twig snaps under foot.
Mother Dragon forms into an ancient oak.
The baby dragons freeze into oak saplings,
their slender branches reaching up to the sky,
dusted with the same golden-green moss as their mother.

You gently touch some of the branches;
You feel them move slightly
before you continue your walk through the forest.

Take the time to explore the ancient forest some more tonight
to see what other forest dragons you can discover…

One… two… three…
It is now time for sleep…
Goodnight and sleep tight!

Meditation 11

The Fairy Tree

Guide Age: 5+
Themes: Celtic mythology, Irish language, embracing talents
Concepts: Summer, flowers, woodland, nature, fairies

This meditation celebrates the First of May in all its splendour and colour. Follow a trail of pink cherry blossom petals to meet a friendly blackbird, listen to a Gaelic song, and be transported into the realm of the fairies. Watch the wee folk as they demonstrate their amazing talents.

This guided meditation provides the opportunity to recognise and embrace individual talents and explore what activities evoke happiness. Help unlock your child's true potential through self-empowerment. This magical adventure nurtures a child's appreciation for the season of summer and promotes an enchanting night's sleep.

Close your eyes…
And take a deep breath…
In through your nose…
And out through your mouth.
In through your nose…
And out through your mouth.

Imagine you are walking through a magical woodland…
Follow the pink carpet of cherry blossom petals
to see where they will lead you.

A red squirrel pops its head up through a pile of petals.
Watch as it scrambles amongst them
and scurries up a nearby oak.

The neighbouring silver birch trees have thin, white bark.
Their low-hanging, vibrant green leaves
dance in the light breeze.

Flute-like birdsong fills the sky overhead.
It is the song of a blackbird!
You spy it perched on the branch of the birch tree.
It has jet-black feathers and a bright yellow beak.
If you look closely, you will see a small yellow ring
around each of the bird's eyes.
The musical verse ends in a swirl of squeaks.
Then the blackbird takes flight.
It lands on the branch of an ash tree, which is
adorned in rich purple flowers.

A melody rises to accompany the blackbird's song.
Feel your body being pulled toward this music…
Stepping forward, you notice a gate up ahead.
You open the gate.
The music leads you into a poppy field.

The melody grows louder and louder.
You spot a solitary hawthorn tree standing in the centre of the field,
its thorny branches clustered in creamy-white flowers.

Words are sung,
but you cannot see who is singing the song.
Listen closely…
There they are! At the base of the tree.

See the fairies in brightly coloured clothes dancing.
They are celebrating the Celtic Beltaine Festival, which marks the beginning of summer.
They start singing the days of the week in their Irish language:

Dé Luain (Jay loo-in)
Dé Máirt (Jay march)
Dé Céadaoin (Jay kay-deen)
Déardaoin (Jay-ar-deen)
Dé hAoine (Jay heen-yeh)
Dé Sathairn (Jay sa-ha-rin)
Dé Domhnaigh (Jay doh-nee)

They invite you to join in:

Dé Luain (Jay loo-in)
Dé Máirt (Jay march)
Dé Céadaoin (Jay kay-deen)
Déardaoin (Jay-ar-deen)
Dé hAoine (Jay heen-yeh)
Dé Sathairn (Jay sa-ha-rin)
Dé Domhnaigh (Jay doh-nee)

Outreaching their hands, they beckon for you to come over.
They want you to enter the tiny door at the base of the tree.
As you step forward, you shrink to the size of a fairy.
The blackbird swoops down, you climb onto its back, and it carries you through the open door and into the Otherworld.

From this great height, you can see many fairies at work.
Some fairies are flying,
some are painting flowers the colour of a rainbow.
You spot a fairy in a beautiful, yellow petal dress collecting the dew from different plants and flowers.
Some fairies are weaving willow twigs into chairs and tables.
One fairy begins singing a different melody.
As she sings a high note, you notice the sun shines brighter;

when she sings a warbling melody, the wind blows.
Nearby, you find a group of fairies sitting cross-legged in a circle sewing and knitting,
and in the centre of the circle, a story fairy recites and acts out a poem.

It is true that fairies have many talents.
You have many talents too.
Perhaps you can sing, dance, play a sport or instrument, write stories, create art, or make people laugh.
Or perhaps, you have another talent.
Think about what you enjoy doing for a moment.
What activities make you happy?

Thank you for sharing! You do have lots of great talents!

Some talents you have discovered already,
and some have yet to be revealed to you.
Throughout life you will learn new things
and develop new talents.
They will benefit the world
and bring happiness to you and to others.

It is time to leave the land of the fairies now.
The blackbird swoops down and carries you on its back through the open door at the base of the hawthorn tree.
You have returned to your own world now.
As you step away from the hawthorn tree,
you grow back to your original size.

The sun sinks beneath the horizon
sending ripples of pink across the sky.
You sit in the poppy field to watch the sunset
and the fairies dance.
One… two… three…
It is now time for sleep…
Goodnight and sleep tight!

Meditations for Unlocking Creativity

Meditations for Unlocking Creativity

How Do These Meditations Work?

The meditations in this section of the book provide the opportunity for your child to experience more creative control within the guided visualisations. They are taught how to unlock their own creativity using their imagination, how to embrace the flow of ideas created, and how to mould and shape these thoughts while embarking on a wonderful journey to an enchanting place, unique to them.

What Are the Benefits of Unlocking Creativity?

By nurturing a child's creativity at night for just five to ten minutes, you will see many benefits; improved self-confidence, increased self-worth, better reasoning skills such as analytical thinking, information processing, abstract thinking and the ability to consider different perspectives. By teaching children how to ignite their imagination at night, role-playing, make-believe games, and storytelling will become more fantastically novel and elaborate during the day as their concentration, positivity, and creative thinking improves.

Positive, creative thinkers are open-minded, more organised, and better at analysis. They can consider an issue in a new way and find alternate solutions, which make them excellent problem solvers. Creative problem solvers make the world a better place.

Creating a Different Focus

These meditations can be particularly useful in shifting focus away from a problem, worry, fear, or even a nightmare. The child's thoughts are refocused to be positive, calming, and happy—a sure way to drift into a contented night's slumber.

Improvise

Take the opportunity to improvise with these meditations. The suggested questions might produce answers that could prompt new and different queries. Follow a child's flow of thoughts and explore the inherent opportunities that are revealed. Avoid simple yes or no questions, instead opting for queries that require more information and detail. This will help the new world to grow around the child.

Meditation Endings

Each meditation ends similarly with a counting exercise, allowing active minds to slow down at their own pace. Vivid and beautiful dreams of adventure are sure to follow.

Meditation 12
Birch Moon

Guide Age: 6+
Themes: Celtic heritage, moon phase, releasing fears and worries, self-assuredness, achieving potential
Concepts: Birch tree, full moon, forest, nature

The birch moon is the first full moon of the Celtic Tree Calendar. It is said to be very powerful, marking a time of new beginnings and giving you a gentle push forward to achieve your goals. All you need to do is let go of any worries or fears that are standing in your way.

This meditation is a great one to share on a full moon and even more magical if shared during the first full moon of the year.

Close your eyes…
And take a deep breath…
In through your nose…
And out through your mouth.
In through your nose…
And out through your mouth.

Imagine you are walking barefoot through a magical forest...

You feel the soft earth beneath your feet
as you pass by trees...

Many ancient trees grow within this forest;
some are hundreds of years old.
Oak, alder, willow, hazel, hawthorn, and ash...
Each of the trees holds secrets and has individual energies.
When you are close to these trees,
you may gain strength, healing, foresight, wisdom, love, or protection.

You look up at the night sky
and notice a trillion stars shining down upon you.
A brilliant full moon captures your gaze.
This is the light that rules the night.

As you gaze up at the moon, you notice the shadows on its surface.
The longer you look, the brighter the moon becomes.

Something heavy is weighing you down.
Strange... You didn't feel it until just now.

You put your hands into your pockets
and take out the rocks that you find.
Hold them up to the moon...
The light of the full moon turns them grey.
These rocks contain all the worries and fears that have been weighing you down recently and
standing in the way of your dreams.
It is time to let them go.
Drop them onto the forest floor.
You do not need to carry them with you anymore.

The moon's light reveals a path in front of you.
Step into the light of the moon.

Feel that magical light wash over you and guide you through the forest.

You are ready to welcome what it is you want to create and achieve.

Visualise what that is.
What would you like to create or achieve?
Keep it in your mind for a moment…

You continue your journey through the magical forest until you come to a magnificent birch tree.
You stand before it.
Notice its silvery bark is peeling to reveal new bark underneath.
It stands tall.
Its slender branches reaching up to the sky
as if it is trying to touch it…
Silver in the moonlight, the tree looks enchanted.
You step forward and touch the birch tree and
feel its soft, papery bark in your hands

Look up… Up at the night sky…
Know that there are no limits for you.
You can do anything you want to do,
be anything you want to be.
You are clever.
You are capable.
You can create anything.
You can achieve anything.
All you have to do is believe in yourself
and know how special you truly are…

One… two… three…
Under the light of the full birch moon,
It is now time for sleep…
Goodnight and sleep tight!

Meditation 13

Flower Friends

Guide Age: 6+
Themes: Friendship, Gardening
Concepts: Garden, flowers, butterflies, bees

Recognising qualities to look for in a friend creates healthy, happy, and longer lasting friendships. Understanding, too, what wonderful qualities you have to offer can promote confidence and increase self-worth. This meditation is set in a magnificent garden bordered by citrus trees, where butterflies frequent in search of nectar and flowers are picked based on their qualities.

Facilitate a growing interest and love for nature by intertwining details from a previous day's gardening session (planting flowers or fruit-picking) or nature outing (butterfly/fruit tree/flower identification). There is also an option here to improvise and ask the child other questions about what they see in the garden around them.

Close your eyes…
And take a deep breath…
In through your nose…
And out through your mouth.
In through your nose…
And out through your mouth.

An archway of trees appears in front of you!
Walk through to see what is on the other side…

Suddenly, you find yourself in a beautiful garden!

As you begin to explore,
you spot fruit trees bearing apples, pears, oranges, and lemons.
Which fruit would you like to pick?

Notice the gooseberry and blackberry bushes have been trimmed into different shapes.
There is a spiral staircase-shaped bush that reaches up to the clouds.
What shapes do *you* see?

Listen! The bees are buzzing close by…
You stop to watch the colourful butterflies as they flutter past.
They are all in search of the tastiest nectar. You follow them…
They lead you to some of your favourite flowers.
Can you name three or four of them?
These flowers are growing in the friendship flowerbed.

Each flower has a special quality that you would like in a friend.

You are going to pick some flowers now.
As you pick each one, tell me what quality you would like in a friend and what flower you feel represents this quality.
(*For example, you might want a cheerful friend, so you pick a buttercup*)

(See page 60 for examples)

It's good to have different friends with different qualities.
You can never have too many friends in this life,
so always keep your heart open to making new friends.

What kind of friend do you think *you* are?
What flower do you think would most represent you? Why?

I know you are a great friend.
You have many friends,
and you are going to have many more in the future.
Anyone is lucky to have you as their friend; I'm sure of that.

You are now standing in the centre of the garden.
There is a beautiful vase. Can you describe it?
What material is it made from? (*Pottery, glass, plastic, gold…*)
Place your flowers in the vase. Take a moment to admire them.

Where else would you like to explore in the garden?
(*The fountain, the herb garden, the aviary…*)

Afterwards, you find yourself beside a yellow rose garden.
Yellow roses symbolise friendship, joy, and happiness.
Breathe in the sweet scent of these roses.
Breathe in happiness. Feel it spread through your body.
I wonder how many roses are in this garden.
Tell me in the morning how many you were able to count.
Goodnight and sleep tight!

Examples of Qualities

Adventurous	Clever	Generous
Brave	Confident	Kind
Bubbly	Creative	Quiet
Calm	Daring	Patient
Caring	Energetic	Shy
Cheerful	Funny	Studious

Examples of Flowers

Buttercup	Heather	Poppy
Bluebell	Herb Robert	Primrose
Clover	Iris	Rose
Cornflower	Lavender	Snowdrop
Daisy	Lilac	Sunflower
Forget-me-not	Lily	Tulip
Foxglove	Marigold	Violet

Meditation 14
Fairy Doors

Guide Age: 4+
Themes: Fairies, imagination, forest, counting, realising talents
Concepts: Trees, fairies, performing

    Magic and performance are at the heart of this meditation. The child creates their own woodland where trees are embellished with fairy doors. The wee folk then appear and extend an invitation to enter through a door of their choice.

    There is an option here to alter the meditation when a different fairy door is chosen the next night. Will the tour of the fairy tree always lead to a tea party? Or will you end up in the throne room, the sports hall, or the garden? Ask questions to uncover details while following the child's train of thought.

Close your eyes…
and take a deep breath…
In through your nose…
And out through your mouth.
In through your nose…
And out through your mouth.

Imagine you are standing in a woodland.
Can you see the flowers growing around you?
What colour are they? Do you know the names of any?

Can you see the different trees in front you?
Can you describe them? What size are they?
What colours do you see?

Look down the trunks of the trees and notice the differently coloured fairy doors.
There are some high up and some down low.
Some of the doors are big and some are small.

What colour is the fairy door you are looking at now?
The door is opening!
A fairy has come out.
Can you describe what they look like? What are they wearing?
While studying your fairy, you notice other fairies
coming out from other fairy doors.
They beckon you to follow them back through their doors.

Take some time to choose which one you will follow.
Which one did you choose?
When you choose, they will tell you their name.
Listen carefully…
What name did they whisper to you?

Suddenly, you shrink to the size of a fairy.
Your back begins to tingle…
You have grown wings!

Follow the fairy through their door now…
Take care. You will have to use your new wings!
You are now inside the fairy tree.
What do you see?

Excited, they lead you to the flying room where you can practice your flying skills.
Lots of other fairies are practicing there too.
Will you practice with them?
How will you test your new wings?

Your fairy friend wants to take you to their favourite room.
You follow them through a corridor.
There is an orange door.
The fairy opens it and enters; you follow.
Describe what you see in this magical room.
What do you think the fairies do in this room?
Why do you think it's their favourite room?

Next, the fairy wants you to join them for a tea party
in the rainbow room.
In this colourful room, you find a long table with lots of sweet treats.
What kind of desserts can you see?
Lots of their fairy friends are there too.
Can you describe some of them?

After you have some food and drink,
the fairies want to perform!
What kind of show do they put on for you?
Is it funny or sad? Does it have lots of energy?
Is there any music?

They invite you to perform next. What an honour!
Think for a moment about all the amazing talents you have.
Then choose one to show the fairies.
When you finish, they all clap and cheer!

It is now time to return to the woodland.
When you leave the tree,
you feel your back tingle as your wings disappear!
You have now returned to your original size.

You might like to visit a different fairy and their door another night.
But how many fairies are there in this wood?
Watch and count the fairies as they go back inside their doors.
Tell me in the morning how many you were able to count.
Goodnight and sleep tight!

Meditation 15
Woodland Adventure

Guide Age: 4+
Themes: Adventure, woodland animals, friendship
Concepts: hedgehogs

Experience what it may be like to be a hedgehog wandering through a woodland. This creative meditation constructs a connection to nature, reinforcing the message to care for and love all creatures on our planet.

Perhaps the child might like to be a different woodland animal another night, such as a fox, squirrel, or otter. Take the time to ask questions to uncover details while following the child's train of thought. Tweak the meditation accordingly.

Close your eyes…
And take a deep breath…
In through your nose…
And out through your mouth.
In through your nose…
And out through your mouth.

Look down at your feet…
They are tiny and furry!

You have a narrow snout
and a round body covered in spikes.
What might you be?

Yes, a hedgehog!

Imagine you are a hedgehog toddling through the woods.
The leaves are under your feet.

Where do you think you are going?

What woodland friends do you meet?

You are feeling peckish.
What do you think you might snack on?

Suddenly, you hear a noise from behind.
What caused the noise? (*Woodland friend, foe, other…*)
What do you do?

Hedgehogs love to explore.
Where do you think you would go next?

You are tired after the adventure.
Where do you think you should curl up to rest?

As you drift off to sleep,
you begin to dream about hoglets toddling through the forest.

Tell me in the morning how many hoglets you were able to count.
Goodnight and sleep tight!

Meditation 16
Wand Wood

Guide Age: 5+
Themes: Celtic heritage, Celtic mythology, magic
Concepts: Ash, hawthorn, hazel, oak, rowan, willow, forest

This meditation, steeped in Celtic tree mythology, unleashes the power of the forest by showing the strength and variety of the trees that grow within it. These trees are the dominant lifeforce within the forest, upon which many ecosystems depend.

Your child may wish to return to this meditation another night to make a different wand. Other wand options can also be added such as birch (ideal for love spells) or alder (spells that restore balance to situations).

This is a magical meditation to do after a walk in the forest. Perhaps you could even make a wand during your next visit!

Close your eyes…
And take a deep breath…
In through your nose…
And out through your mouth.
In through your nose…
And out through your mouth.

Imagine you are walking through an enchanted Celtic forest with the aim of finding the perfect wand...

But to find the perfect wand, you must first think of the type of magic you wish to create.

To help you, here are some of the trees within this forest and their unique properties:

Ash
- Used for creative spells
- Can perform miraculous healings
- Can strengthen friendships
- Used for spells involving the higher spirit realm.

Hawthorn
- Used for Fairy Magic
- Used for spells of mischief or of kindness, you decide.
- Can be used to open the gateway to the otherworld

Hazel
- Used for channelling wisdom into spells
- Used for the power-of-good spells

Oak
- Used to channel strength into your spells
- Can call on the power from the otherworld, making them extremely powerful

Rowan
- Perfect for love and protection spells
- Grows on the sacred border between mountains and land, allowing you to gain access to visions of the future

Willow
- Used for purification spells, renewal, and healing.
- Can harness the power of nature.

ᛜ Grows on the sacred border between water and land, allowing you to use either of these elements in your spells

Which tree do you choose to make your wand out of? Why?

Now it is time to find your tree in the forest.
I will tell you where to look…

Ash
Travel to the edge of the forest where you will find humble ash trees growing together. Look for oval leaves and grey bark. Place a leaf in your pocket to enhance your creativity and welcome friendship.

Hawthorn
Look on the outskirts of the forest, in the middle of the meadow. Look for red berries! Place one in your pocket for love.

Hazel
Under the canopy of oak and ash, look for rounded leaves and smooth brown bark. Don't forget to place a hazelnut in your pocket for wisdom.

Oak
Oak trees grow in the heart of the forest. Look for acorns. Place one in your pocket for strength.

Rowan
Rowan trees are also called mountain ash. These trees grow in mountains and connect heaven and earth. You must climb the mountain to reach them. Look for the red berries! Place one in your pocket for protection.

Willow
Willows grow on the sacred border between water and land. You must walk toward the river. Look out for long leaves and elegant branches dipping into the water! Take a small piece of willow bark for healing.

Once you've found your tree, select and cut a small branch from it
to make your wand.
Are you ready?

Now, think of all the spells
you are going to cast with your new wand.
Tell me in the morning which spells you cast.
Goodnight and sleep tight!

Meditation 17
Snail Trail

Guide Age: 5+
Themes: Discovery, foraging, caring for small creatures
Concepts: Fruit tree, orchard, snails, birds

This meditation allows the child to walk in the shoes of a forager and discover the fruit of a new tree that lies deep in a wild orchard. Botany, ornithology, and code-breaking features in this unique adventure.

Perhaps you might visit another night and discover a different fruit tree. There is an option here to improvise and go in search of a new species of flower, plant, or animal!

This is a beautiful meditation to do after a walk through an orchard or a morning spent fruit-picking.

Close your eyes…
And take a deep breath…
In through your nose…
And out through your mouth.
In through your nose…
And out through your mouth.

You feel a hat on your head…
You are wearing this bucket hat to protect you from the strong rays of the sun.
What colour is it?
Does it have a pattern on it? If so, describe it.

You can also feel garden gloves on your hands…
What colour are they?
Do they have a design on them? If so, describe it.

You are dressed like a gardener!
What else are you wearing?

You are not only a gardener, but an expert forager of wild plants! And you are about to go in search of a new fruit tree that grows deep in the wild orchard.

Excited to uncover what awaits you, you start walking down a path.
On one side of the trail, there are nut trees.
What type of nut trees can you see?
You see a furry creature run between the trees. Small animals love to forage for nuts.
What types of animals do you see?

On the other side of the path, you find bushes with plump berries.
What types of berries are there?
You hear the twittering of songbirds. Birds love to forage for berries.
What types of birds do you see?

On the path in front of you,
You notice a small rock.
Suddenly, it begins to move!
It's a snail, which appears to be following the slimy trail from another snail…
And another snail…
And another!

You look at the path ahead that twists and turns through the bushes and trees…
And you spy the snail trail stretching into the distance.
Where do you think the snails are going?

The path forks into two directions.
You continue to follow the snail trail.

Some of the snails are in the centre of the path.
They could dry up in the hot sun or get stepped on.
You decide to pick them up with your special gloves and place them onto nearby plants.
As you lift one of the snails, you notice that it is very colourful and has a pattern on its shell.
Can you describe the colour and the pattern?

It's odd… It is a secret code!

You look around to see if anything else in the orchard matches the snail's pattern.
You spot a tree with similar colours and patterns!
This tree is a gateway into a magical land.
You put your hands on the trunk of the tree and a portal opens.
You step through… Tell me about this land and what you see…

After your adventure, you return to the path of snails.
These snails are travelling slowly.
It will take them time to reach their destination,
but they are determined and have patience.
When they need a friend to help,
they have you to pick them up.

Sometimes when you want to do something,
it might take a while to learn
or reach the place you want to go to.
Sometimes, there will be a problem
that you might need to solve.

When things get tough,
sometimes, you can get through it on your own,
and sometimes you might need family or a friend to help.
Be patient.
Be determined.
And you will reach your goal
Just like the snails.

Finally, you have reached the end of the snail trail.
The snails have led you to the wild orchard!
All the trees have juicy fruits that you recognise.
What kind of fruit do you see?
As you walk deeper into the orchard, you
search for the new species of fruit tree.
There it is!
Describe the tree…
And its fruit…
This is the first time this fruit has ever been discovered!
What will you name the new tree and fruit?
You really *are* an expert forager.

As the wind blows through the branches of this tree,
the fruit moves, creating music.
The tree lowers its branches for you
and welcomes you to pick its fruit.
You spy a basket and a new pair of gloves nearby.
You change your gloves and lift the basket.

Pick the fruit one-by-one off the branches
until you fill your basket.
Tell me in the morning how much fruit you were able to pick.
Goodnight and sleep tight!

Meditation 18
A Walk through an Enchanted Forest

Guide Age: 5+
Themes: Celtic heritage, culturally-significant trees, happiness, self-assuredness
Concepts: Elder/hawthorn/holly/crab apple trees, forest

This meditation draws on Celtic tree mythology to introduce messages of self-worth and foster a strong connection to nature.

There is an option here to improvise and ask the child other questions about their surroundings and/or to visit more Celtic trees like the ash, a magical tree that spans between worlds, or birch—a tree symbolising transformative change and new beginnings.

Close your eyes…
And take a deep breath…
In through your nose…
And out through your mouth.
In through your nose…
And out through your mouth.

Imagine you are walking through an enchanted forest…

You look down to see that you are barefoot.
There is a carpet of soft leaves beneath your feet.
Can you describe what you see around you?

You are searching for our native trees.
These trees have been around for thousands of years,
and our Celtic ancestors believed each tree had a unique energy…

Your journey starts here…
First, you pass under the elder tree.
The elder tree is known as the tree of healing and regeneration.
If you ever feel hurt or if things don't go to plan,
know that you have the ability to recover and
rise up stronger than before.
Always listen to your inner voice.

Your journey through the forest continues…

What kind of animals do you think live in this forest?
Can you see any of those animals?

Next, you pass by the holly tree…
This tree symbolises peace and goodwill.
From kindness comes peace and harmony.
Think of something kind that you did for someone lately.
Tell me about it.

Can you remember a time when you were happy for someone who
did something well?
Tell me about it.

Know that kindness spreads happiness.
You have the power to brighten someone else's day.

A small bird lands on one of the holly branches.

Can you describe the bird?

Next, you pass under a crab apple tree…
This tree is known as the tree of youthfulness.
Know that you can always be young at heart,
Feel the simple joys through the different seasons…
The sound of birdsong in early spring,
the smell of a sweet rose in summer,
the sight of the colourful tumbling leaves of autumn,
the taste of a cinnamon hot chocolate in winter.
Allow yourself to feel happiness when faced with the simple joys of life and you will always feel young.

You continue through the forest…

Can you see the babbling brook up ahead?
Have a look into the water.
What do you see?

Farther into the forest, you pass under the cherry tree…
This tree symbolises beauty and love.
You are beautiful.
You have love in your heart.
Know that the love of family and friends will always surround you, giving you strength when you need it.
The branches are covered in white cherry blossoms.
Petals begin to fall,
showering love upon you.

Now, reach up and touch the petals as they drift from the branches…

Tell me in the morning how many petals you think fell from the tree.
Goodnight and sleep tight!

Meditation 19

Monkey Puzzle

Guide Age: 6+
Themes: Adventure, friendship, exploration
Concepts: Trees, jungle, chasing dreams, monkeys

Swing through the jungle as a mischievous monkey in this meditation and visit a cave or venture to the far side of a waterfall.

This meditation encourages the development of friendship through fun and laughter and imparts upon the child the necessity to follow dreams, no matter how big or small.

Close your eyes…
And take a deep breath…
In through your nose…
And out through your mouth.
In through your nose…
And out through your mouth.

Imagine you are a monkey swinging from tree to tree.

You are looking for the tallest tree,
The lookout tree!
When you find it,
you nimbly move your arms and legs,

scaling to the very top.
From there, you can see the entire jungle.
Can you see any animals below? Which ones?
What are they doing?
Do you notice anything else from the lookout spot?

Happy with your journey,
you decide to climb down.

Imagine what some of your friends
might look like if they were monkeys.
It's time to monkey around!
What trick would you play on your monkey friends
to make them laugh?
Can you think of any games you might play with them?
Isn't it great to have fun with friends?

Now, it's time to explore the jungle!
Where would you like to go?

Eventually, you decide to swing through the trees…
To your left, you spot a cave,
and to your right a waterfall.
Would you like to explore the cave
to see what's inside?
Or travel behind the rushing waterfall?

(What do you find in the cave?)
(What do you find behind the waterfall?)

It's time to explore some more!

You swing through the trees
In search of the Monkey Puzzle Tree.
This tree is said to be a challenge
as it's difficult to climb,
even for monkeys.

But you are an expert climber.
If you have big dreams or aspirations,
they might seem out of reach right now,
but know that if you work toward them in small steps,
you can reach them.
You can do anything you want to do,
be anything you want to be.
All you need to do
is believe in yourself!

It's now time to climb the Monkey Puzzle Tree!
Wait!
Before you climb,
tell me what kind of puzzles you like…
(Mazes, crosswords, riddles, sudoku, jigsaw, wordsearches, codebreakers)
What do you like most about those types of puzzles?

Now, it is time to begin the fun and challenging climb
up the Monkey Puzzle Tree!
Count the branches as you go and don't stop
until you reach the top!

Tell me in the morning how many branches you were able to count
on the way up.
Goodnight and sleep tight!

Meditation 20
Alpine Forest

Guide Age: 6+
Themes: Pine trees, train journey, family, mountains, adventure
Concepts: Train, pine trees

Family is at the heart of this meditation where together you embark on a train journey through a pine forest. You arrive at a quaint village in the mountains. The main adventure in the village is imagined by the child. A breathing exercise is followed by the soothing sounds of the train on the tracks, lulling the child to sleep.

There is an option here to improvise and set the scene as a Christmas train, adding snow and all things festive, so the child can build their own Christmas adventure.

Close your eyes…
and take a deep breath…
In through your nose…
And out through your mouth.
In through your nose…
And out through your mouth.

Imagine you are standing on the platform at a train station with your family.

Down the tracks,
a train appears in the distance.
Clickety-clack, clickety-clack.
Watch as the train draws closer and closer along the tracks.
Finally, the train pulls into the station
to come to a gradual stop.

Describe what the train looks like.
(Colour, shape, size, how many carriages, etc.)

It's time to board!
Climb up the steps into the carriage and look for a seat.
When you find one, your family follows and sits next to you.
Tell me when you are sitting comfortably.

The train's horn sounds,
and it suddenly chugs into motion.
As it pulls out of the station,
you look out the window.
Describe what you see.

Going on a trip with family
creates memories that can be cherished forever.
You must have already saved up lots of memories
of your trips together.
Can you think of a recent trip you took?
Can you think of a fun or happy memory from that trip?

It's time to continue this nighttime adventure…
The train begins to climb the tracks
that lead up to the mountains.
You spy a pine tree forest.
When you look more closely at the trees,
what do you notice?
(Are there birds, animals, or other plants growing?)

The train stops at a mountain village.

You disembark with your family
and follow the path up to the village square.
See the trees decorated with twinkling lights?
Reindeer are wandering past.
The air is cool and crisp.
What else can you see?
(Stalls selling goods, the smell of certain foods, the sound of church bells, etc.)

You have some time to explore the village.
Tell me what you see as you walk.
(Children playing, musicians, festive decorations, cafes, shops)

It is time to board the train.
You make your way down the path.
As you breathe in, the fresh scent of pine fills your lungs.
And with each exhale, you feel more and more relaxed.
Breathe in calm, breathe out and relax.
Breathe in calm, breathe out and relax.

You have now reached the platform.
It is time to board the train with your family
and find your way back to your seat.
The train's horn sounds,
and it chugs into motion.
Travelling home on the train, you hear the
Clickety-clack, clickety-clack
of the railway tracks.
You feel your body sway gently with the motion of the train.

Clickety-clack, clickety-clack, clickety-clack…

Your body is becoming more and more relaxed.
Count the clickety-clacks until you drift off to sleep.
Tell me in the morning how many clickety-clacks you were able to count.
Goodnight and sleep tight!

Meditation 21

Your Very Own Tree Adventure

Guide Age: 5+
Themes: Whatever you want it to be in relation to trees!
Concepts: Whatever you want it to be in relation to trees!

This meditation is created solely by the child.

Begin with a breathing exercise to promote relaxation:

Close your eyes…
And take a deep breath…
In through your nose…
And out through your mouth.
In through your nose…
And out through your mouth.

Ask some general questions to help the child visualise themselves in their own adventure. Some example questions to get you started might be:

Where are you?
What are you wearing?
What can you see?
What are you doing?

If your child needs help getting started, introduce a subject that interests them, such as:

Forest Creatures	Ants Badgers Bats Bears Birds Deer Earthworms	Foxes Hedgehogs Insects Rabbits Squirrels Wolves Woodpeckers
Forest Plants & Trees	Brambles Celtic trees Ferns Moss Mushrooms	Native trees Nettles Wildflowers Toadstools Vines
Activities	Adventuring Dancing Hiking Mountain Biking Running	Singing Thrill Seeking Treasure Hunting Treetop Trails Ziplining
Science	Astronomy Botany Exploration Forester Geology Geography Habitat Conservation	History Ornithology Palaeontology Research Time travel Zoology
Magical Creatures Living in Forests	Centaurs Dragons Elves Fairies Giants Kelpie	Phoenix Trolls Unicorns Werewolves Warlocks Witches

As the child begins to build a creative world around themselves, you can ask specific questions to add detail. Avoid asking any leading questions as the aim is to allow the child to be in control.

The outcome is a wonderful adventure of their very own creation, a great way to exercise their imagination and open their mind to free-flowing thoughts.

Acknowledgements

There are a number of people who made this book possible. I wish to extend my sincerest thanks for their support and encouragement.

My three saplings—Willow, Hazel, and Rowan—who continue to inspire me every day. I am so proud to see their interest and appreciation for the world and nature grow continuously. Without them, this book would not exist.

My amazing husband, Stephen, who supported me by giving me the space and time to create this book. Your patience and encouragement are forever appreciated.

My nature-loving mother, Aine, who first introduced me to the beauty of the natural world and who still enjoys her walks by the riverbank and strolls on the sand.

My editor, Kara Wilson at Emerging Ink Solutions, for her enthusiasm, encouragement, and expert advice. Thank you for being with me on this journey. The book series, *Bedtime Meditations for Children*, would not be the same without you.

And finally, to my readers and those of you who asked for another meditation book—thank you for your continued support. I hope you enjoyed the book.

About the Book...

My love and appreciation for trees was cultivated from a young age by my nature-loving mother. She would bring my siblings and me on nature walks where she would identify wildflowers and trees. She was just sharing her passion for nature, not realising the positive effects it would have on our future lives.

The meditations in this book were created for my three saplings—Willow, Hazel and Rowan—and were based on subjects they love. The inspirations came while on family walks in beloved Irish forests, parks, hillsides, and mountains. Some ideas were inspired by childhood memories of walks with my own mother and tales of fairies that my grandmother shared.

Identification of wildflowers and trees is a favourite pastime of my children now, and they enjoy visualising them in the meditations. It brings them happiness and peace and, in turn, a restful night's sleep. I wanted to share our tree collection of meditations with other families. I hope this book brings them joy.

About the Author...

Ann Margaret Walsh lives in Dublin with her family. She studied both Science and Communications at university and has worked in many exciting roles within these fields. She has been on countless adventures around the world and always wants to travel and explore more places. Children's education, well-being, and nature are particularly important to her and feature strongly in her books. She has a passion for nature photography, which she regularly shares on her social media channels.

Printed in Dunstable, United Kingdom